Rosie and Friends
Positively Different

Written by
Helen C. Hipp

Illustrated by
Taryn Cozzy

Edited by
Paula Tedford Diaco and Susan Lackey

About the Author

Helen Hipp has had her own kind of safari through the land of a large family. She was always exploring new ways to define herself. There are many ways to navigate the waters of life says Helen. "You may ride in a canoe, sailboat, motorboat, or you may find yourself on the back of a pink hippo!"

With a mindset that centered on creating opportunities out of obstacles, Helen explored career opportunities, by connecting her personal experiences (parenting a child with special needs) with her beliefs, professional skills, and aspirations.

Helen received her M.A. in counseling and began her career as a psychotherapist to help people find answers for their life problems. Her work eventually evolved into a coaching practice, WithinU Life Coaching, focusing on individuals with special needs and their families.

Helen has authored articles for Family Works and Washington Family Magazine and written multiple self-help articles published by ezine.com where she is viewed as an expert in her field. She has been a contributor as a special needs consultant to FOX44 News in Burlington, Vermont.

Her debut children's book, *A Different Kind of Safari*, released in 2013 puts into words the essence of Helen's teachings—addressing the many questions life asks by offering up lighthearted, ever-changing perspectives that transform personal challenges into opportunities. Once again, the engaging safari family led by Rosie the Pink Hippo inspire, and help you see your life differently in her new book, *Rosie and Friends Positively Different*.

Meet Rosie!

Dedication

This book is dedicated to my father, Thomas Ludlow Chrystie; my mom, Eliza Balis Chrystie; and son, Raymond Gordon Chadwick, II. Their positive outlook and use of personal challenges in meaningful ways reflect the essence of this book.

Contributions and Acknowledgements

A special heartfelt thank you to family and friends for their support and encouragement.

Note to Parents and Educators

This book is a creative and fun teaching tool intended for parents, caregivers, teachers, and children who may have felt at some point in their life that they were different from their peers.

Rosie and Friends Positively Different
Copyright,© 2016 Helen C. Hipp, M.A. CTACC
Publisher, A Different Kind of Safari, LLC
ISBN 978-0-9890134-2-0

An explorer of sorts, Rosie the pink hippo often wonders what it would be like if she had been born a gray hippo and looked like all the other hippos in her pod.

What if there was only one way of doing things? Would every single hippo be doing the same thing the same way? Rosie asks herself. "What if I could no longer see or experience differences. How would I learn?"

Rosie cannot imagine wanting
to live in a world like that!

Never the same or boring, Rosie sees her life as positively different.
Being different gives Rosie a good reason to celebrate her differences
every day, a good reason to enjoy being herself, always learning,
always exploring!

Just as if he had heard her thoughts, a monkey swinging from a
branch overhead asks,
"Why is celebrating your differences so important?"

Startled, Rosie realizes she's been talking out loud and many animals are eagerly listening to her. More than just a few playful monkeys gather around. An elephant with small ears, a lazy lion, a miniature giraffe, an ostrich, and a restless rhino walk over to join the crowd, too.

Curiosity is contagious, Rosie thinks.

Eager to know what Rosie knows, the monkey repeats his question.

"Why is celebrating your differences so important?"

"Celebrating your differences is important because differences encourage us to explore new places, people and things. They play a part in making the world an interesting and more colorful place."

"Don't you have to be important, win a medal, or have a birthday to have a celebration and to be celebrated?" the Elephant asks.

Nodding in agreement, it appears that the other animals also have the same question.

"Enjoying and celebrating yourself is about more than an event," Rosie says. "It is about accepting your strengths, uniqueness, and weaknesses. What is important when planning your celebration is for you to share what you feel good about."

"So if you feel happy on the inside it is celebrated on the outside?" asks the Elephant.

"Is it kind of like turning yourself inside out?" Rhino asks.

Pointing out that they each see things differently, Rosie answers "yes" to both the Elephant and Rhino.

She is reminded of her one-of-a-kind friends Eli-zee, Ray, and TLC, known as the Tender Loving Crocodile, who also see things in many different ways.

Rosie's friend Eli-zee, who is a zebra with a distinct look, steps out from the crowd, surprising all who had not seen her.

Eli-zee, who does not want her new friends to be fearful of her ability to hide, does the unexpected. She teases them by disappearing in and out of the brush like a magician, reciting again and again, "Now you see me, now you don't," until a nervous ostrich interrupts the game with a question.

Feeling vulnerable the ostrich asks, "But when you are noticed, and seen as different, how do you get others to see you the way you see yourself?"

"How others see you depends mostly on how you see yourself," Eli-zee says, looking into a puddle of water.

The ostrich waits patiently for Eli-zee to continue.

Realizing their friend is too busy admiring her own reflection to talk to the ostrich, TLC and Ray, who have been quietly listening, chime in.

"Ostrich, we are all similar in some ways but different in others. Awareness and courage are needed to recognize your own uniqueness and capabilities. So don't worry about being modest. How do you really see yourself?" Ray asks.

"I think . . . I think . . . I do not know!" the ostrich stutters.

Baffled and embarrassed, the ostrich tells her new friends,

"I . . . need a while to think."

"Take all the time you need," TLC says gently.

Then something clicked!

No longer feeling nervous, her friends have helped her realize that she can choose to see herself differently. She had only needed to give herself permission to be herself. Uniquely different from any other type of bird, Olivia the ostrich now sees herself as an exotic bird that is positively different!

"What about you Rosie? How do you see yourself?" Olivia asks.

"And when do you get to celebrate yourself?" asks the elephant.

"Positively different is how I see myself, and when to celebrate myself, why not right now?" Rosie says, breaking into her celebration song.

Celebrating My Differences ~ Differences

Is what my song is all about

So sing along and let your happiness out!

My Differences ~ Differences

Instead of following the beat of the drums like some, I like

My Differences ~ Differences

Unknown and strange in my jacket of pink. Such an oddity is wonderful, don't you think, for a hippo so pretty, to also be pink!

Should it matter what other gray hippos may think,

When I like

My Differences ~ Differences!

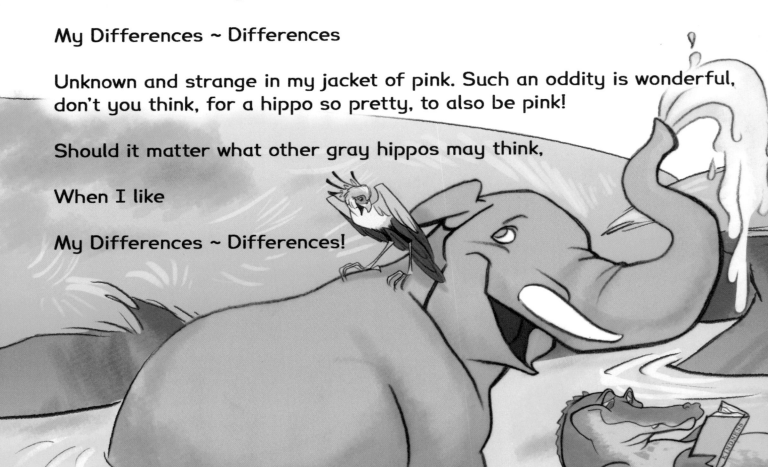

THUMP
THUMP
THUMP

Positively Different
I am...

Unusual
. . . different in a way that is interesting or unexpected

Exotic
. . . because I am different from what is ordinary

Colorful
. . . because of a one-of-a-kind uniqueness

Positively Different
We Are!

Unusual
... different in a way that is interesting or unexpected

Exotic
... because we are different from what is ordinary

KINDNESS

Colorful
... because of our one-of-a-kind uniqueness

Celebrate in Song by Sharing Your Unique Self!

Everyone has a story to share. When thinking about celebrating yourself, what kind of thoughts come to mind?

Using the template below, fill in the blanks using one of the words in brackets to create the introduction and chorus to your song. What is it about you that you want to celebrate and sing about? Write about you.

Celebrating Differences ~ Differences
Is What (My, Our) _____ Song Is All About.
So Sing Along, And Let Your Happiness Out!

(My, Our) _____ Differences ~ Differences

Instead of following the beat of the drums like some, (I, we) _____ like
(My, Our) _____ Differences ~ Differences

Positively different . . . (I am, or we are!)
Just say it and sing it!

_____
_____
_____
_____

When (I, we) _____ like (my, our) _____
Differences ~ Differences

Rosie asks, "What advice would you give your friends who want to feel better about themselves?"

The End

Want to spend M⊕RE time with Rosie and Friends?
Visit her online @ RosieTheHippo.com!

CPSIA information can be obtained at www.ICGtesting.com
Printed in the USA
BVIW12n0129241017
498476BV00002B/2

* 9 7 8 0 9 8 9 0 1 3 4 3 7 *